I0451816

Praise for Storyshares

"One of the brightest innovators and game-changers in the education industry."
— Forbes

"Your success in applying research-validated practices to promote literacy serves as a valuable model for other organizations seeking to create evidence-based literacy programs."
— Library of Congress

"We need powerful social and educational innovation, and Storyshares is breaking new ground. The organization addresses critical problems facing our students and teachers. I am excited about the strategies it brings to the collective work of making sure every student has an equal chance in life."
— Teach For America

"It's the perfect idea. There's really nothing like this. I mean, wow, this will be a wonderful experience for young people."
— Andrea Davis Pinkney, Executive Director, Scholastic

"Reading for meaning opens opportunities for a lifetime of learning. Providing emerging readers with engaging texts that are designed to offer both challenges and support for each individual will improve their lives for years to come. Storyshares is a wonderful start."
— David Rose, Co-founder of CAST & UDL

Invisible Fences

Storyshares presents

Published by Storyshares, LLC
Inspiring reading with a new kind of book.

Storyshares
Storyshares, LLC
24 N. Bryn Mawr Avenue #340
Bryn Mawr, Pennsylvania 19010-3304
www.storyshares.org

Interest Level: Late Elementary
Grade Level Equivalent: 3.7

ISBN 9798885976831
Book design by Saskia Globig

Invisible Fences

Thomas Rameaka

Storyshares

Contents

Chapter One

When I opened the front door after school that day, I knew something was wrong.

I could hear my parents arguing. They almost never argued. And my dad was home. He was *never* home when I got off the bus.

Another weird thing was that our dog, Dillon, wasn't there to greet me. Usually, as soon as my feet hit the front step I could hear his greeting. It was an excited mixture of yelping, barking and whining. It was like he hadn't seen me in months instead of a few hours.

As soon as I opened the door, he was ready to knock me down. He'd slobber me with kisses with his front paws on my chest, his tail wagging a hundred miles per hour.

This time, though... nothing. It was complete silence. Until I heard my mom and dad. Then, I heard Dillon's name. Their voices had that tone that spelled trouble.

I leaped three steps at a time and skidded to a stop in our kitchen. Mom and Dad sat at the counter. They stared at me like I had just broken a window or something. I looked from one to the other.

"Where's Dillon? You didn't give him back to Wendy, did you?"

My dad let out a huge sigh and just shook his head.

"Dillon's at the dog pound. This is the *second* time this month. They caught him wandering around Rita's yard. And how come he keeps losing his collar? This has to stop."

"It's not his fault!" I protested. "All he does is wander over to Rita's, sniff around and come right back. She just spots him in her *precious* yard and immediately calls the pound. He hates his collar. It won't stay on unless I really cinch it tight. Then he starts breathing funny.

"What is with her? Rita doesn't even tell them Dillon lives right next door! C'mon, Dad, we have to go get him. No dog should spend even a minute in that dog jail."

My dad slowly stood up. He put both hands on my shoulders and said, "Not this time, Patrick. We don't pick him up until you and your brother come up with a plan. Then, you *talk* to our next-door neighbor. She doesn't bite. She's just afraid of dogs."

Ugh. Talk to the old woman who never came out of her house except to harass our gentle dog.

"But Dad..."

"No *buts*. Then, and only then, do we pick Dillon up from the pound."

It was my turn to sigh. I walked slowly down the hall to tell Nate the bad news. I knew I'd find him on the floor surrounded by Legos. He'd be totally unaware of what was going on with our *other* brother, Dillon.

Chapter Two

I should tell you a little bit about our dog, Dillon.

Nate and I had been begging for a dog for a long time. My parents had been planning a move from our old house for about a year. They agreed that we could get a dog when we found a bigger house. Nate and I thought they were just stalling. We were sure they thought we'd get busy or distracted. After all, we were *always* busy.

We spent most of our days at school and riding our Big Wheels on our sloping driveway. We both loved basketball. We couldn't wait for our own hoop. Hopefully, on a new, flat driveway.

But we also talked all the time about getting a dog. Nate wanted a German Shepherd. He loved that they were also called police dogs. He told anyone who listened that he wanted to join the poice force when he grew up. He had plenty of time to change his mind. He was only in kindergarten.

I really didn't care about the breed. I was almost three years older than Nate. I knew my parents wouldn't *buy* a dog. Definitely not a purebred like a German Shepherd.

"We'll adopt a pound puppy when we move," my dad announced at dinner one night.

Every Saturday for the past year or so, Nate, me, and my dad would visit the local animal shelter. Dad always told Mom we were going to the playground. We did go, but only after stopping by the pound to "browse."

As soon as we drove in the parking lot all the dogs started to howl, yip, and whimper. It's as if they knew this was the family that could spring them from dog jail.

We would circle around back where the dogs coud be seen in their fenced runs. Many looked sad, like they had given up even wishing to leave and become someone's pet. Some, however, looked excited, barking up a storm.

To me, each bark sounded like *"Take me home, take me. Take me!"*

Others just growled. It was like they were just plain angry that this stinky dog pound was where they ended up.

Then a crazy, amazing thing happened. My dad found an ad in the local paper:

9 month old English Setter. Free to good home. Owner going back to school and cannot care for it. Must interview. If interested call Wendy at 860-429-0888.

"We have to be interviewed?" my mom chuckled.

Mom's family never had a dog. She grew up with three brothers and three sisters. I don't think her parents could imagine adding a dog to the mix.

Dad, on the other hand, loved dogs. Even though he was one of six kids, they had several dogs over the years. They even had a St. Bernard! Dad's parents probably thought, *How much crazier can it be?*

Dad was definitely on our side.

"I'm still not sure these boys are old enough to have a dog," Mom added. "It's a huge responsibility. Are they going to walk it every day? Brush it? Feed it? Pick up its poop?"

That last one drove Nate and I into a fit of giggles. Dad quickly jumped in.

"Honey, we'll *all* take on the responsibility. It will do the boys good to have to take care of something else. As far as the poop goes, we live on the edge of acres of woods. We'll walk him there. We can train him to do his business in the woods, too.

"All those walks will also get us into shape! You'll see, having a dog will be work, but also a lot of fun. Plus, it's a *purebred* Setter! Only nine months old! It's probably already halfway trained."

Mom looked at me and Nate. It was the same look she always gave us when we *swore* we had brushed our teeth before bed. Like she could read our minds.

"Okay, call this Wendy woman. Set up a visit. But I swear if that dog jumps up on me or slobbers on me, it's no deal."

I could barely sleep that night. All I could think about was getting our own dog. I pictured taking him for long walks in the woods. He would curl up next to me by our fireplace. I could tell him all my secrets and he'd never repeat them to anyone.

Chapter Three

Wednesday finally arrived. It felt like the day before Christmas. Only a dog would be the best present I ever got.

I kept looking at the classroom clock. Was it broken? *Why did it move so slow?*

My teacher, Miss Baker, noticed my clock watching.

"What's going on, Patrick?" she asked. "You're usually the first one done! Those math problems are not going to solve themselves." Five minutes later, she called me up to her desk.

"Okay, what's the matter with you today?" she asked.

I blurted out, "We're going to get a dog after school today! It's an English Setter. I... I just can't concentrate."

Miss Baker smiled and started writing something on a small piece of paper.

Oh no, I thought, *she's writing a note to my parents!*

Before I could open my mouth, she handed it to me.

"Take this pass down to the library. I want you to jot down all the facts you can find about English Setters." She smiled and added, "I remember my first dog, too. The cutest beagle you ever saw. We named her Tammy."

My feet barely touched the hallway floor. I floated down to our school library.

The library was one of my favorite places. It had big shelves full of books. Hundreds of them, of all shapes, colors and sizes. And they were filled with tons of information. There was no better feeling than holding a book in my hand.

I'd never been out of New England, where we lived. But books transported me to exotic places. Many clear across the world. Some even to the deepest parts of the ocean, like *Journey to the Bottom of the Sea.*

I loved to read. I mean, really loved to read.

I kept a flashlight under my pillow at home. My parents called for lights out every school night around 8:00. They used to want me to shut down at 7:30. I always pleaded for one more chapter and they always gave in. Finally, we all settled on 8:00.

As soon as they closed the door, out came my book and my flashlight. Funny, I never remembered closing my book and putting the flashlight under my pillow. But there they were every night, back in place. Weird, huh?

I gave Mrs. Richardson, the librarian, my note. She showed me a shelf that was full of animal books. There seemed to be every breed of dog in the world on this shelf. I found one that had the title, *English Setters: Bird Dog Supreme*.

Huh, "bird dog?" Never heard of such a thing. I began reading. There were some hard words here and there but I decoded them. "Decoded," that's what Miss Baker always called breaking a word into its parts and sounds.

I took out my notebook and jotted down as many facts as I could. I wished I could spend all afternoon reading this book. But I knew I only had about twenty minutes. Here's what I wrote:

- English Setters came from England. *(I know, like, duh.)*

- English setters were bred to fetch ducks and other birds shot by hunters. *(Really? Not sure how I felt about that)*

- They are called "bird dogs." *(Reason? See above)*

- They have big lips and soft mouths. This is to help carry the birds back to the hunter. *(Hmm...)*

- They love people and are very friendly and loyal *(Yes! Everything I want in dog! And a friend!)*

Chapter Four

Long story short, we adopted Dillon.

Just Dad, me, and Nate went to Wendy's place to be "interviewed." Mom missed out on the jumping up and slobbering part.

I could tell right away that Dillon was the dog for us. Wendy, his owner, told us he was a Laverack Setter. This meant he was bigger than the smaller hunting Setters. Laveracks didn't mind not hunting and were happy being family dogs.

Perfect! I thought.

Dillon was also called an Orange Belton. This was because he had a lot of orange spots and patches on his coat.

We all fell instantly in love with him. He ran around Wendy's yard, fetching sticks and playfully rolling around with us. I think he knew we were the family for him. And Dad was right about his training. He sat on command. He'd even run back to you when you called him.

I did feel bad for Wendy, though. She had returned to college. She could not give a nine-month-old puppy the time he needed. I think she felt happy that Dillon was going to a family. Four of us would shower him with attention.

I saw tears in her eyes as she handed the leash over to Dad. Looking at Dillon's eyes, he seemed sad, too. It took him a few days, but he settled in as our fifth family member. It really was like we had gained another brother.

But we still had a problem to solve.

I slowly walked into Nate's room. Being in different grades, he always got home before me. As usual, he had Legos spread all over the floor. He looked up as I said, "We have a huge problem."

"No," he said. "I have a huge problem. I can't find the one Lego piece I need to finish this."

He held up a Lego construction that had

THOMAS RAMEAKA

pieces sticking out all over the place. I had no idea what he was building.

"Uh, right. I'll help you with that later. This is way more important. Mom and Dad didn't tell you?"

"Tell me what? Wait. Dad's home already?"

Typical, I thought. *Nate's been home for hours. And I'm the one who gets blamed for Dillon's wandering! Again.*

"Dillon's in the dog pound," I said. "Yeah, Rita again. Dad wants us to come up with a way to keep him from leaving the yard. We can't just put him on the run and forget about him."

Nate looked like he was about to cry. "She's a mean old witch. She hates everything except that ugly black cat of hers! Whenever we play basketball she slams her doors and windows. I think she would send us to the dog pound if she could!"

Wow.

Nate was the so-called "quiet brother." I was the one always getting sent to my room for opening my big mouth. My dad always said, "Patrick, you could talk the skin off a ten-foot snake." I could not remember Nate stringing that many sentences together at once.

25

"Yeah," I said, "I agree. Last week I got lucky. I caught Dillon just as he crossed onto her property. And there she was. She stood about ten feet away from us. She held that mangy cat of hers, Ruggles or Riggles or whatever she calls him.

"They *both* looked at me with these hateful, squinty eyes. The cat's hair was up on his back. Dillon wagged his tail and grinned like a goofball. I thought he was going to roll over and ask them to scratch his belly. It was like he found some new buddies."

"I love Dillon," said Nate.

"Yeah, we all do. And Dillon loves *everyone*. That's part of his problem. He's not scary enough. He should have growled, showed his teeth and chased that ugly cat up a tree!"

"And Rita with her," muttered Nate. "So what did she say?"

"Rita told me, 'Keep that mutt off my property! If I see him again I'm going to tell the dog pound to put him down.'"

"What did she mean, '*put him down*?'"

"She means have him put to sleep. Forever! And do you want to know the worst thing? Today is the *next* time!"

Chapter Five

Nate and I sat on the floor in his room. We always thought better when we were building with Legos. I was still trying to make an airship I saw in our favorite movie, *Star Wars*.

"So, any ideas?" I asked, snapping another piece in place.

"What if we just *talked* to Rita? Mrs. Luce, my teacher, always says it's better to talk than fight. I can tell her that Dillon is a sweet dog. Tell her he'd never hurt her cat," said Nate.

"Really, Nate? *Talk to her?* After what she said about telling the dog pound to put him to sleep? I never want to talk to her again. Are you crazy? Don't you remember last Christmas?"

Nate tossed a blue Lego in the pile.

"Yeah, but that wasn't Dillon's fault. Rita just opened the door and dropped her cat on his head!"

I closed my eyes and shook my head. The memory was still fresh in my mind.

Mom had made a big batch of her famous holiday brownies. I mean, they were so tasty! She covered them with green frosting and then poured melted chocolate on top. Everyone begged her for the recipe after they had one bite.

Nate, being the sweet brother, asked Mom if we could bring some over to Rita. This gave Dad a great idea. Or, what he *thought* was a great idea.

"Yes! That's it, Nate! Not only will we bring Rita a dish of brownies. You will deliver them with me. And here's the smart part: You, Nate, will be holding Dillon on the leash.

"Rita will see how well-behaved Dillon is. She'll be amazed that he's so gentle that a *kindergartener* can handle him with ease. Plus, we'll butter her up the with the best-tasting brownies on Earth! A foolproof plan!"

Nate seemed pleased that his idea had gotten Dad all excited.

I just rolled my eyes. I was also the "glass half empty" brother.

The next day, our kitchen smelled like the sweetest chocolate. Mom put a batch of brownies on a holiday-colored paper plate with a big red bow. I gave Dillon an extra brushing. He looked like a show dog.

I whispered in his ear, "This probably won't work. Make sure you don't shake your head and slime Rita."

Part of me wanted Dillon to do just that. He was the king of slobber. The first time he met our Aunt Carol he shook his head when she bent down to pet him. Slobber flew off his lips and landed right on her nose.

Aunt Carol screamed like she had been slapped! Nate and I fell down, we were laughing so hard.

Nate looked very nervous. He never was the one who took Dillon on a leash for his daily walk. Dillon was pretty strong. It was usually Dad and I that were dragged down the street.

"Just let him know who's boss, Nate," said Dad.

"Yeah, and say his name loud and firm," I added.

"Okay, you two," Mom said, "Nate will handle Dillon just fine. Right, Nate?"

Nate let out a soft, "Right."

I crossed my fingers as they headed over to Rita's. I ran to watch them through the side window.

Our two houses were separated by trees. In the winter, with the leaves all down, we had a perfect view of Rita's front door. There was a hard, icy snow on the ground. It was mid-December, and only a few inches covered her lawn. She hadn't yet scraped it off her front steps.

Nate seemed to be handling Dillon pretty well. I didn't see him pulling on the leash really hard. I think Dillon sensed he had a small person holding the leash. Just another example of what a sweet dog we had.

Dad was a few steps behind them, holding the plate of brownies. I held my breath. *Here goes nothing.*

Dillon hopped up Rita's front steps. Just as he got to her door, it suddenly flew open. Obviously, Rita had not seen her visitors arrive on her front steps.

My eyes opened wide, and before I could even scream, Rita dropped her beloved black cat right on Dillon's head!

The window was closed. I couldn't hear

anything. But even now, if I close my eyes I can still picture it. It was the most horrible and funny thing I ever saw.

The cat landed on Dillon's head like a big owl snatching a little field mouse. For a few seconds it looked like they were in shock and didn't move a muscle. Then all hell broke loose!

The cat's claws dug into our poor dog's head. It must have screeched. The cat, of course, did not wish to be dropped on a dog's head. And Rita did not want her cat dropped on Dillon's head. But there it was.

It looked like Dillon was wearing a horrible black cat Halloween hat on his head. Half cat, half dog. Just as quickly, the cat leaped off. It ran between my dad's legs.

This caused Dad to slip on the icy snow. Trying to keep his balance, he flung the brownies up in the air.

Dillon whirled around and chased the cat up the nearest tree. There were two problems. First, the nearest tree was about twenty feet across Rita's yard. Then there was the second problem.

Nate never let go of the leash!

The icy yard made the perfect sliding surface. Nate and Dillon looked like a weird run-away bobsled. By this time, Nate was flat on his tummy.

I think he was actually laughing. I could see his mouth open with a big smile on it. He thought this was a riot! He was having a blast being pulled across Rita's yard.

Dillon finally stopped at the base of the tree. As he put on the brakes, Nate went flying off into some bushes. Only then did he let go of the leash. Dillon was barking so loud I could hear him through the closed window.

The cat just looked down him from a branch of the tree. It seemed to be smirking at Dillon.

Can't get me now, can you? Stupid dog!

Chapter Six

So much for trying to butter Rita up. I was convinced it would take all the butter in the world to do that.

Dad picked up all the brownies while Rita kept yelling at him. She told him to catch that vicious dog and get him off her property. She threatened to sue us if our "out-of-control mutt" (yes, she called him a *mutt*!) touched one hair on poor little Riggles' body!

Dad tried to tell her about the gift we were giving her. He held the messed-up brownies out to her. A peace offering. Rita just grabbed her cat and slammed the door in his face.

Nate, meanwhile, climbed out of the bushes. He grabbed Dillon's leash again. Even Dillon looked ashamed of himself. He followed Nate back to our house hanging his sore head. It wasn't even his fault!

Mom and I met them at the door. She had her hand over her mouth, trying not to laugh. But when she saw Nate's and Dad's faces, she just said, "I hope you guys have a Plan B."

Two days later, we had a new plan. Dad gathered us around the computer. He found this thing called "The Invisible Fence."

It showed a guy burying a wire around the outside of a yard. He placed it completely around the area you wanted the dog to stay within. Then he connected the wire to a power source. He demonstrated how to turn it off and on.

Your dog had to wear a special collar that would give a small jolt of electricity if he crossed over that wire. He went on to say that the jolt would never really harm your pet. It would be just enough to "remind" him not to leave the yard.

Dad assured us this company sold thousands of these each year. Once a dog experienced a couple of shocks, that usually did it.

Dillon would never go outside of the backyard and into Rita's yard again. He'd have the full run of our backyard surrounded by the "Invisible Fence." We wouldn't have to put him on a run or his leash anymore. It would also keep him safe.

We all talked it over. We agreed, as Mom said, there were more pros than cons. None of us wanted to see Dillon get shocked. But none of us wanted him to run out in the road and get hit by a car. And we definitely did not want to bail him out of the dog pound again. Or have to deal with our grouchy next door neighbor.

The first time we put Dillon in the backyard with his new "shock" collar, I almost cried. He tried to follow us to the front yard and immediately got zapped!

He yelped and ran to the middle of the yard. He just sat there, trembling. He looked at us like we had utterly betrayed him.

Dad told us we all had to be patient with Plan B. Nate and I spent a lot of time coaxing Dillon away from the middle of the yard. We played with him and gave him dog treats. He would take some little steps at first.

At last he seemed to understand. After a couple more shocks, he avoided the areas with the buried or invisible wires.

Even though it worked, it didn't mean Nate and I had to like it.

Things calmed down after that. Dillon did not go to the pound. We avoided getting in trouble with Rita.

One night, at the dinner table, Nate asked Mom and Dad a question.

"Do all old people live alone?"

Chapter Seven

"Do all old people live alone?" Nate asked.

"No, dopey," I said. "Billy's grandparents live in another part of their house."

Billy was in Nate's grade. He lived across the street with his parents and his mom's folks. We all played together. We even made a cool fort. It was hidden in the woods behind our house. His parents worked, so his grandparents took care of him a lot.

Dad had his mouth full of pizza, so Mom spoke up, "Stop calling your brother names. No, Nate, most elderly people live with a spouse. You know, a husband or wife. Many live with a partner or friend. Some live with their children. Many live in a special home for the elderly."

"Grandpa lives by himself," I said, grabbing another piece of pizza.

"So does Rita," said Nate.

That caused a moment of silence. We rarely talked about Rita since the invisible fence was put up in our yard. It was like Rita became invisible to us, too. It made me think of another saying: "Out of sight, out of mind."

Dad wiped his mouth with a napkin. He still had some red sauce on one side of his mouth.

"Guys, Grandpa used to live with Grandma until she died. You boys remember Grandma, right?"

Nate and I both nodded.

It was weird, but I barely remembered Grandma. She died when I was almost five and Nate was two. I remembered her being very old and frail. She couldn't move very well. She was the only Grandma we knew, since Mom's mother and father died before we were born.

"Rita lives by herself," Nate continued. Once he got an idea or a question in his head, he never gave up.

"Rita had a husband," said Mom. "I chatted

with Mrs. Kelley, not long after we moved here. Remember, she lives on the other side of Rita. I mentioned what a character Rita was. She told me Rita's husband died about fifteen years ago. She raised both her kids by herself. They're all grown up now and live pretty far away."

Wow, Rita was married and had kids.

For real? I thought. *What else didn't we know about Rita?*

"If she's a mother, why is she so grouchy and mean all the time? You're a mother and you're almost never grouchy." Nate saw the surprised expression on Mom's face. "Oh, and you're *never mean*," he added quickly.

Mom smiled at this and said, "You never know what other people's lives are like. We don't know a lot about Rita. She keeps to herself. I don't know how we'd cope if anything happened to any of you. Maybe I would become grouchy and mean."

I thought about Rita and her slamming the door in Dad's face as he held out the brownies. How could you get to know anyone who stayed in her house all the time?

Back to Mom's comment about becoming mean and grouchy. *No way!* Mom was too nice and loved being around people.

She was "taking a break," as she called it, from her job. She wanted to wait until Nate was in school for a full day before going back. She didn't stay in the house all day. She and a few of her friends met at the park a few times a week.

Sometimes she even took Dillon with her to the park. The other women had dogs, too. Mom said it was important that Dillon hang out with other dogs. She said he needed to get away from the invisible fence once in a while.

She reminded us about a dog in our old neighborhood. She was a Pit Bull mix. Her name was Sugar and she was anything but sweet. Her owner kept her tied by a chain to her dog house most of the day.

I loved dogs. But I was scared to death of Sugar. She would snarl, show her teeth, and look like she was going to break the chain holding her every time someone walked by.

Mom said dogs are like people. If you treat them with love and respect, they usually give it right back.

I thought again about Rita. I didn't know if Mom meant *all* people or just *most* people.

I had an idea. "Why don't we ask Grandpa to come live with us?"

Mom glanced at Dad with a look of panic on her face.

I was really getting into this idea. "Nate could move into my room. Grandpa can take over Nate's room."

Nate's eyes lit up. "We can have bunkbeds! And I can bring all my stuff into the new bedroom! Oh, right," he added sheepishly, "and then Grandpa wouldn't be lonely."

Wait a minute. All his stuff? He had a lot of stuff! And what about my stuff? Would Nate be constantly getting into it?

Now I wasn't so sure about my idea.

"Uh, that's a really nice thought, Patrick. I'm sure Grandpa does get lonely sometimes. But he would never go along with it. He's too independent," Dad said.

"And opinionated!" Mom said, closing the pizza box.

"Well, and that," admitted Dad. "I think he's real used to being on his own now. He'd have a hard time living with a family again."

"Maybe that's why Rita doesn't like us," I said.

Nate, Mom, and Dad looked at me like I had two heads.

"Rita doesn't like us?" asked Nate.

Nate thought life was forever going to be like his kindergarten. A place where everyone hugged each other and held hands while singing songs like "The more we get together, the happier we'll be..." Anyone disliking him just did not compute.

"Rita doesn't dislike us!" Dad almost jumped out of his seat. He settled back down and added, "I mean... She just... she just likes her space."

"And unfortunately, our family dog invaded that space once too often," said Mom.

"It's like she wants a forcefield around her, like the alien movie we watched," said Nate. "I saw her out by the end of her driveway yesterday. She was chopping the ice around her mailbox. It wasn't very cold out, but she had her whole face covered. It was like she thought if her face was covered up, no one would recognize her or something."

I thought about that. It kind of made sense.

"Yeah, like Jimmy Bouchard," I said.

Jimmy was a seventh grader who wouldn't let anyone sit with him on the bus. He lived on one of the few farms in our town. His house looked pretty broken down. His driveway was filled with old tractors and car parts.

He always just made the bus. He'd get on the bus and say the same thing to the driver every time: "Chores, again." The driver just nodded. Billy would go to the very back of the bus. He'd shuffle to a seat that no one else dared sit in.

He wore the same jeans and flannel shirt to school almost every day. There was also a faint whiff of manure around him. He had his own forcefield. He also sat by himself in the cafeteria in school. If anyone even looked like they wanted to sit with him, his scowl kept them away.

Suddenly, it seemed everywhere I looked I was thinking about one thing.

Invisible fences.

Chapter Eight

That January, it seemed we had a huge snow-storm every week. Dillon was let out in the backyard a few times a day. He'd roll around in the snow. He loved eating it.

His face looked so funny when his slobber turned into icicles. Even with his warm fur, the cold drove him back in the house after about ten minutes.

Dad had bought a new snowblower. The snowstorms in New England were intense. Sometimes shoveling was out of the question.

We loved it when we heard the sound of the snowblower starting up. We got in our snowsuits and ran outside. We loved to stand in the yard as waterfalls of snow shot over our heads.

Dad taught us how to dig deep into the piles he left behind and make igloos. We'd bring Dillon inside with us. We'd pretend we lived in the Arctic and he was our trusty sled dog.

After he was done blowing our driveway, Dad always did Rita's, too. I thought he was trying to butter her up after all the grief Dillon caused.

He just said, "No person over the age of sixty-five should be trying to shovel their own driveway. Hiring a plow is just too costly. Plus it's the neighborly thing to do."

He came back in the house one Saturday after finishing both driveways. He looked like a snowman. The wind had blown the snow back on him and covered him with a light coating.

"I don't think Rita's home. The whole house seems shut down and her car is gone. In fact, I think she's been away all winter. Probably went someplace warm."

"Her daughter lives in Florida," said Mom, pouring hot cocoa into mugs for all of us.

Again, it seemed weird thinking of Rita as

a mom. I wondered if she tucked her kids in at night and read them bedtime stories. I was getting older but still loved that nightly routine. I wondered if Rita still read her daughter bedtime stories when she stayed at her house.

Another week came along with another big snowstorm. We tried to make a snowman, but the snow just wasn't sticky enough. Dad plowed our driveway and then Rita's. I wondered if when Rita came home she'd think some magic elves had shoveled her driveway. I asked Dad why he bothered with Rita's since she wasn't home.

"You don't want the snow to pile up too high. If it gets above four feet or so, even a snowplow might have trouble getting through it. Plus, when Rita does get home, she'll be able to get her car back up the driveway."

All the houses on our side of the street stood at the top of a steep hill. Our driveways were long and uphill.

I loved going down and getting the morning paper in the winter. I would just sit on my bottom and the ice would do the rest. The trip back up, though, was hard. I had to walk on the side of the driveway in the deep snow. No way could I make it up to the top without slipping. But the ride down was definitely worth it.

Then something happened that seemed to change everything. Just when I thought I had everything figured out, one event turned things upside down. By things, I mean the way we all felt about Rita.

I stepped off the school bus at the usual time. I geared up for the long climb up our icy driveway. That's when I saw something that did not belong in our neighborhood. At least, I never saw one here before.

An ambulance!

It was just pulling away when I noticed something else. *Mom!*

She was waving goodbye to the ambulance as it slowly pulled away from Rita's driveway.

Huh?

She held Dillon by the collar.

Dillon? Don't tell me he got caught in Rita's yard again!

Mom and Dillon walked slowly up to me. I noticed she didn't have a jacket on. She must have left the house in a hurry.

I couldn't understand why an ambulance came here. Who was hurt? And why was Dillon out of the yard? He still had his special shock collar on.

But how did he...?

I looked at Dillon again, then saw Mom shivering in the cold.

Mom saw my confusion. "It's a long story. Rita got hurt. C'mon, I'm freezing. I'll tell you all about it when we get back inside. Here, take Dillon."

Dillon really didn't need me to hold on to him. He was shivering, too. I let him go and he sprinted for the front door. I held on to Mom as we made our way back up to the house.

I couldn't wait to hear *this* story.

Chapter Nine

Mom refused to tell me any details until I had taken off my boots and coat. Finally, we were all seated at the kitchen counter. She already had some water heating up for hot cocoa. By this time, Nate had joined us. He looked as confused as me.

"Did Dillon bite Rita? Is that why the ambulance had to come?"

Mom looked at Nate like he was speaking a different language.

"Dillon, *bite* Rita? Ha! You know he doesn't bite!"

Then she said something that made our mouths drop open.

"This dog here," she said, kneeling down and hugging Dillon, "is a hero!"

"Whaaat?" we both yelled at once.

"Yup. Your beautiful dog saved a life today!"

Nate and I looked at each other and we both burst out laughing. "How? Who?" I asked.

Mom's answer shocked us both.

"Rita. Dillon saved Rita's life today."

Nate and I sat stunned for a few seconds.

"I thought Rita was in Florida?"

"She came home late last night," Mom said, as she poured hot water over the cocoa mix in the mugs. "Settle down, relax, and I'll tell you all about your hero dog."

The story mom told made me think of one of those animal adventure movies. All we needed was some popcorn. Nate and I just sat for the next ten minutes or so. We both wore hot cocoa moustaches as the story unfolded.

Mom told us she let Dillon out into the backyard around 2:30 that day. It was the usual time she let him out to get some fresh air and do his business.

"I got busy doing some stuff in the house. I honestly forgot about him. Usually, he barks or whines at the back door when he's ready to come in. It must have been about a half an hour before I opened the door and called for him.

"I looked around the yard from the back deck and still didn't see him. I checked to see if the power on the invisible fence was still working. The green light was blinking away."

"You mean... Dillon ran *right through* the electricity? *He took the shock?*"

Nate and I looked at each other with wide eyes.

Holy moly! He never took the shock!

He hated getting shocked. Ever since that first day with the fence. He always stayed about six feet away from the perimeter of our yard. Even when we were shooting hoops on the driveway.

"Yup, he took the shock because Rita was in trouble." Mom took a long sip of her cocoa.

She went on to tell us that she heard a far-off barking. It seemed to come from down the street.

At first, she didn't think it was Dillon. He never was a big barker. But Mom knew Dillon's bark. It had to be him down the street. She ran back inside, got into her boots, and went down the driveway to investigate.

"As I got closer to the street, the barking got louder. It was definitely Dillon! It sounded so urgent. I walked into the middle of the road because the snowdrifts were so high. Finally, I spotted him.

"At first I thought he was hurt. He was lying on the ground. Then I noticed something strange. Someone had their arms around him. And they were not letting him go!"

"Rita was *hugging* Dillon?" I asked. "The same Rita who wanted him put to sleep?"

"Yup, one and the same. In fact, I had to almost pry her arms off him! I think he's her new best friend. He was not only keeping her warm, he was sounding the alarm."

"Sounding an alarm?" asked Nate.
Mom told us that she noticed Rita clenching her teeth and wincing. Then she noticed Rita's foot. It looked like it was lying at a funny angle. She went to touch it and Rita almost screamed.

"I think it's broken!" Rita had cried. "I've been out here for almost an hour. Thank goodness your dog found me! I was getting colder by the minute. I felt like I was going into shock. My goodness, what a gentle creature that dog is. He allowed me to snuggle right up and his body heat did the rest."

Mom said Rita kept gabbing away. "It was

like she hadn't talked to another human in weeks. Plus, it seemed to keep her mind off her ankle."

Mom immediately called an ambulance on her cell phone. She never let that phone out of sight. Luckily, it was in her back pocket when she raced outside. While they waited, Rita told Mom what happened.

"She said that she got in from the airport very late. She couldn't believe that someone had thought to plow her driveway. She worried the whole way home that she'd have to leave the car and her luggage on the street all night. When I told her that your father had been snowblowing her driveway all month long, she couldn't thank me enough.

"She had come down the driveway this afternoon to shovel out her mailbox. Just as she got near it, her feet flew out from under her. That's when she fell and broke her ankle."

"And that's when our hero came along to save her!" Nate said.

"And ran right through the invisible fence!" I added, looking down at Dillon.

He had his eyes closed. His loud snores made us all laugh.

The craziest thing was that Dillon never went to the dog pound again. It was crazy because later we told Rita about the Invisible Fence.

She insisted that we take it down that day.

About the Author

Tom Rameaka is a retired school teacher who loved reading and writing with his students every day. He lives near the coast of North Carolina with his wife, Mary, who is also a retired teacher. Tom and Mary have two grown sons and five grandchildren. The family had many happy years with their English Setter, Dillon.

About the Publisher

Storyshares is a publisher focused on supporting the millions of teens and adults who struggle with reading by creating a new shelf in the library specifically for them. The ever-growing collection features content that is compelling and culturally relevant for teens and adults, yet still readable at a range of lower reading levels.

Storyshares generates content by engaging deeply with writers, bringing together a community to create this new kind of book. With more intriguing and approachable stories to choose from, the teens and adults who have fallen behind are improving their skills and beginning to discover the joy of reading.
For more information, visit storyshares.org.

Easy to Read. Hard to Put Down.

www.ingramcontent.com/pod-product-compliance
Lightning Source LLC
Chambersburg PA
CBHW071226170626
46809CB00005BA/1949